GREAT FAIRY TALE CLASSICS

ILLUSTRATED BY TONY WOLF
TEXT BY PETER HOLEINONE

© DAMI EDITORE, ITALY

Published by Tormont Publications Inc.
338 Saint Antoine St. E.
Montreal, Quebec
CANADA H2Y IA3

Printed in Italy

Printed by Officine Grafiche De Agostini S.p.A.
Bound by Legatoria del Verbano S.p.A.

The story of
CINDERELLA
and other tales

Once upon a time . . .

. . . there lived an unhappy young girl. Unhappy she was, for her mother was dead, her father had married another woman, a widow with two daughters, and her stepmother didn't like her one little bit.

CINDERELLA

All the nice things, kind thoughts and loving touches were for her own daughters. And not just the kind thoughts and love, but also dresses, shoes, shawls, delicious food, comfy beds, as well as every home comfort. All this was laid on for her daughters. But, for the poor unhappy girl, there was nothing at all. No dresses, only her stepsisters' hand-me-downs. No lovely dishes, nothing but scraps. No nice rests and comfort. For *she* had to work hard all day, and only when evening came was she allowed to sit for a while by the fire, near the cinders. That is how she got her nickname, for everybody called her Cinderella. Cinderella used to spend long hours all alone talking to the cat. The cat said,

"Miaow", which really meant, "Cheer up! You have something neither of your stepsisters have and that is beauty."

It was quite true. Cinderella, even dressed in rags with a dusty grey face from the cinders, was a lovely girl. While her stepsisters, no matter how splendid and elegant their clothes, were still clumsy, lumpy and ugly and always would be.

One day, beautiful new dresses arrived at the house. A ball was to be held at Court and the stepsisters were getting ready to go to it. Cinderella didn't even dare ask, "What about me?" for she knew very well what the answer to that would be.

"You? My dear girl, you're staying at home to wash the dishes, scrub the floors and turn down the beds for your stepsisters. They will come home tired and very sleepy." Cinderella sighed at the cat,

"Oh dear, I'm so unhappy!" and the cat murmured "Miaow".

Suddenly something amazing happened. In the kitchen, where Cinderella was sitting all by herself, there was a burst of light and a fairy appeared.

"Don't be alarmed, Cinderella," said the fairy. "The wind blew me your sighs. I know you would love to go to the ball. And so you shall!"

"How can I, dressed in rags?" Cinderella replied. "The servants will turn me away!" The fairy smiled. With a flick of her magic wand. . . . Cinderella found herself wearing the most beautiful dress, the loveliest ever seen in the realm.

"Now that we have settled the matter of the dress," said the fairy, "we'll need to get you a coach. A real lady would never go to a ball on foot!"

"Quick! Get me a pumpkin!" she ordered.

"Oh of course," said Cinderella, rushing away. Then the fairy turned to the cat.

"You, bring me seven mice!"

"Seven mice!" said the cat. "I didn't know fairies ate mice too!"

"They're not for eating, silly! Do as you are told! . . . and, remember they must be alive!"

Cinderella soon returned with a fine pumpkin and the cat with seven mice he had caught in the cellar.

"Good!" exclaimed the fairy. With a flick of her magic wand . . . wonder of wonders! The pumpkin turned into a sparkling coach and the mice became six white horses, while the seventh mouse turned into a coachman, in a smart uniform and carrying a whip. Cinderella could hardly believe her eyes.

"I shall present you at Court. You will soon see that the Prince, in whose honour the ball is being held, will be enchanted by your loveliness. But remember! You must leave the ball at midnight and come home. For that is when the spell ends. Your coach will turn back into a pumpkin, the horses will become mice again and the coachman too will turn back into a mouse . . . and you will be dressed again in rags and wearing clogs instead of these dainty little slippers! Do you understand?" Cinderella smiled and said,

"Yes, I understand!"

When Cinderella entered the ballroom at the palace, a hush fell. Everyone stopped in mid-sentence to admire her elegance, her beauty and grace.

"Who can that be?" people asked each other. The two stepsisters also wondered who the newcomer was, for never in a month of Sundays, would they ever have guessed that the beautiful girl was really poor Cinderella who talked to the cat!

When the prince set eyes on Cinderella, he was struck by her beauty. Walking over to her, he bowed deeply and asked her to dance. And to the great disappointment of all the young ladies, he danced with Cinderella all evening.

"Who are you, fair maiden?" the Prince kept asking her. But Cinderella only replied:

"What does it matter who I am! You will never see me again anyway."

"Oh, but I shall, I'm quite certain!" he replied.

Cinderella had a wonderful time at the ball . . . But, all of a sudden, she heard the sound of a clock: the first stroke of midnight! She remembered what the fairy had said, and without a word of goodbye she slipped from the Prince's arms and ran down the steps. As she ran she lost one of her slippers, but not for a moment did she dream of stopping to pick it up! If the last stroke of midnight were to sound . . . oh . . . what a disaster that would be! Out she fled and vanished into the night.

The Prince, who was now madly in love with her, picked up her slipper and said to his ministers,

"Go and search everywhere for the girl whose foot this slipper fits. I will never be content until I find her!" So the ministers tried the slipper on the foot of all the girls . . . and on Cinderella's foot as well . . . Surprise! The slipper fitted perfectly.

"That awful untidy girl simply cannot have been at the ball," snapped the stepmother. "Tell the Prince he ought to marry one of my two daughters! Can't you see how ugly Cinderella is! Can't you see?"

Suddenly she broke off, for the fairy had appeared.

"That's enough!" she exclaimed, raising her magic wand. In a flash, Cinderella appeared in a splendid dress, shining with youth and beauty. Her stepmother and stepsisters gaped at her in amazement, and the ministers said,

"Come with us, fair maiden! The Prince awaits to present you with his engagement ring!" So Cinderella joyfully went with them, and lived happily ever after with her Prince. And as for the cat, he just said "Miaow"!

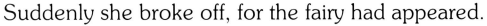

THE SNOW MAIDEN

Once upon a time there was a beautiful garden which became even more beautiful that day, after a heavy fall of snow covered the ground, the trees and bushes in a soft white mantle. A little boy and girl were playing happily in the garden, they were brother and sister.

They chased each other, threw snowballs and played hide and seek under the fir trees. Then the little girl said,

"Let's make a snow doll."

They began to make the doll and decided it would be a girl.

"So there will be three of us and we'll have more fun!" said the little girl. So they carefully built a doll made of snow, with a pretty oval face, long hair, large eyes and a delicate little mouth. It looked just like a real little girl.

"Let's give her a kiss and maybe her lips will turn red like ours," said the sister. So they kissed the doll . . . and lo and behold, its lips turned red!

And the snow doll's cheeks turned pink. When a sudden gust of wind blew from the north, the doll came to life. It moved, smiled at the two children and started to play with them.

Some time later, the children's father returned from town. When he saw the girl in white playing with his own children, he said to himself,

"It must be one of the neighbour's daughters." Then he said to the little snow doll, "Come into the house and get warm." But the snow maiden made a frightened sign as though to say "No!" The man, however led her into the house, saying,

"Oh, you're so cold! The fire will soon warm you up!" But the snow maiden sighed sadly, though she didn't have the courage to speak. In she went and stood by the window, looking out at the white garden. Then she began to weep – and slowly and gently, she began to melt . . . until nothing was left of her except a trace of white snow on the floor. . . .

SAYED'S ADVENTURES

Once upon a time, in the mysterious East, lived a man called
Benezar who married a woman named Zemira. They were in
love with each other and agreed on all things, except one. Zemira
believed in magic, omens, premonitions and fairies. Benezar only
believed in what he could see before his eyes. However, that did
not mar their happiness at all, and this reached its height, when,
one day, in the midst of a thunderstorm, Zemira gave birth to a
handsome baby boy. When Benezar, who had anxiously awaited
the arrival, was allowed to see the baby, he noticed a tiny whistle
hanging from a thin silver thread round its neck.

"What's this?" he asked.

"It's a gift a fairy made to our son," replied Zemira. "It's a magic
gift. Take it," she went on, removing the whistle from the child's
neck, "give it to our son when he is twenty."

"All right. But listen, what are we to call the child?" asked
Benezar.

"Sayed," replied Zemira.

The years went by and Sayed grew healthy, strong and brave. He was eighteen years old when he decided to go on a pilgrimage to the holy city of Mecca. He told his father of his decision.

"Yes, I'm pleased you're going," said his father. "In fact, Sayed, take this as a lucky charm," and he gave him the fairy's gift.

"What is it?" Sayed asked.

"It's a whistle. Your mother, alas now dead, thought highly of it. Carry it with you always."

"I will father," said the young man, putting the whistle round his neck.

Not long after, the travellers with a hundred camels, many merchants and a host of guards, set out on the journey. Young Sayed was splendidly equipped and armed with a sword, spear, bow and arrows.

It was a long, long way to the holy city of Mecca. They travelled over plains, mountains and deserts. It was on a long stretch of desert that they were attacked by a large band of robbers. They were caught unaware, some tried to flee, but Sayed shouted:

"Flee? Where do you think you can flee to in the desert? Come on. Let's die fighting!" and he hurled himself against the attackers. At the height of the fighting, Sayed was attacked by a young robber, richly dressed and riding a white horse. The young man bravely faced his attacker and killed him with his sword. A soldier nearby shouted out,

"What have you done? You've killed Almansor. This is the end, let's run!" Men ran in all directions. Now practically alone, Sayed remembered the whistle round his neck. If it really was magic, it might be able to help him . . . he put it to his lips and blew hard . . . But nothing happened. Not so much as a whisper of sound.

In the meantime, the others had fled. Sayed was taken prisoner, bound and led before Sheik Selim, a very powerful man, the leader of several of the desert tribes and, unfortunately, the father of Almansor, the very man Sayed had killed. Selim, however, was not an unjust man. When he discovered that Sayed had taken Almansor's life in a fair fight, he refused to allow a hair of his head to be harmed. Indeed, he set him free and entrusted the young man to some travellers

about to leave for far off Mecca, the holy city.

Sayed thus found himself once more on his travels. However, one night, friends of the dead Almansor captured him.

"Your master told you not to kill me," cried the young man.

"We're not going to kill you. All we're going to do is tie you up and leave you here in the desert. Thirst and the sun, or the vultures or the jackals will do the rest. They, not us, will kill you!" And laughing cruelly, they rode away. Two whole days went by. Sayed was on the point of death, baked by the sun and with no water, when close by passed some travellers belonging to Kalum the merchant. They came to his aid and saved his life.

As he came back to his senses with the first sips of water, Sayed spoke:

"May Allah reward you, Sir, for saving my life. What is your name?"

"My name is Kalum," said the man, "but it won't be Allah who will reward me. You are going to do that yourself. If I hadn't come along, you would have been dead by now. And you are going to work for me until you have repaid that debt. What is your name?"

"Sayed," he answered.

"Well, Sayed, get up and come with me." The young man went along with Kalum and on the way discovered that he was a rich merchant from Baghdad, so that was the city in which he went to live. At that time, Baghdad was ruled by the famous Caliph, Harun-el-Rascid, wise, valiant and loved by all. Kalum owned a big bazaar in the city and it was there that Sayed was put to work doing all the humble jobs.

One day, a veiled woman came to the bazaar. Sayed was amazed when she said to him,

"You're Sayed, aren't you?"

"Yes," he replied in astonishment. "How did you know that?"

"Tell me, have you still got the whistle round your neck?"

"Of course!" exclaimed the young man. "You must be the fairy who gave it to my mother. But what is this whistle *for*? I've tried blowing it, but . . ." The woman interrupted him.

"It will be of no use to you until you are twenty. Then it will save your life. Now tell me, what can I do for you?"

"Help me to get home," Sayed replied. "I need lots of money for that, which I don't have."

"But you're brave and strong. You can earn it," said the woman, and she explained that, every week, tournaments were held in the city, and Harun-el-Rascid, the Caliph, always watched them. The winners received rich prizes. The veiled woman had weapons, armour and horses and she lent these to Sayed. He took part in the tournaments and always beat the others, winning lots of prizes, as well as the Caliph's admiration. Sayed, however, never revealed his name, but just mentioned that he was a horseman from distant Cairo.

Now it so happens that the Caliph, Harun-el-Rascid, liked to wander through the city at night, disguised as a beggar or merchant, to hear what folk had to say about him. Not to spy on them, but to try and put right any mistakes he might have made. Sometimes, he was accompanied by his chief minister. Well, one night, as Sayed was going home to Kalum's bazaar, he heard shouts and the sounds of struggle. Four men had attacked two others in a dark corner. The brave young man immediately came to the rescue by killing two of the attackers and chasing the others away. When it was all over, the two victims thanked Sayed and asked him,

"Brave youth, what's your name?"

"My name is Sayed," came the reply.

"I'm Kalum the merchant's shop assistant."

"Hmm," said one of the two men, "you seem to be more of a gentleman than a shop assistant. However, take this ring as a reward for what you did for me." Then the other man spoke,

"And this bag of coins. You've saved my life and you deserve it. Goodbye!" And away they went.

Sayed stood there with the ring and bag in his hand. With these he could now find a ship and go home.

Next day, he said to Kalum,

"I'm leaving. I shan't be working for you any longer."

"And where are you going to?" asked Kalum.

"Home!" answered Sayed.

"Home? But it's a costly journey, and with the wages I pay you . . ." Sayed smiled,

"Your pay certainly wouldn't take me far, but . . ." and he held out the bag, "but this money will. Farewell!" However, wicked Kalum was not to be defeated. He told the police Sayed had stolen a bag of gold. The young man was immediately arrested. The chief of police asked him,

"Who gave you this money?"

"A man I'd never seen before," was the honest reply. Sayed was judged a thief and sentenced to deportation to Thirsty Island, the home of the worst kind of criminals. On the ship the young man thought to himself, "Well, I left home two years ago, proud, rich and happy. Here I am today, twenty years old, in the midst of these convicts, condemned to live and die an innocent man in prison!"

During the night there was a terrible storm. Driven by the wind, the ship was flung about by the waves until it crashed onto some hidden rocks.

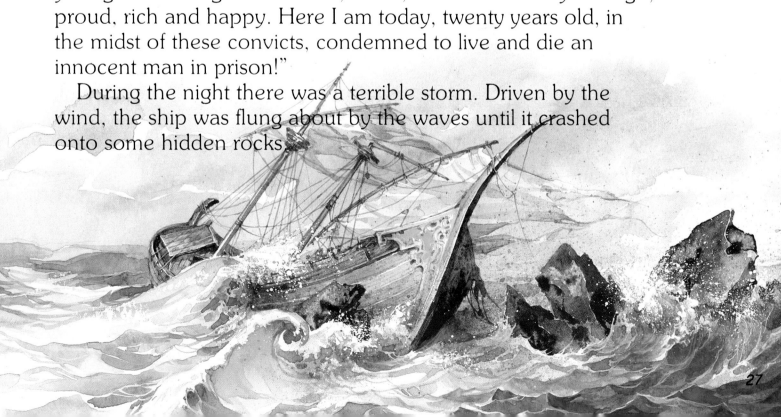

Only one man survived the disaster. It was Sayed. At the
mercy of the waters, he groped for something to hold on to, but
nothing came within his grasp, until he suddenly felt his fingers
touch the whistle the fairy had given him. Desperately, he blew
it . . . and a dolphin surfaced beside him, shaking its head as
though to tell him to get onto its back. Sayed clambered up and
there found safety. He remembered the fairy had told him that
when he was twenty years old, the whistle would save his life!
The dolphin carried the young man within sight of land.

"Thanks, friend!" called out Sayed as he slid down from the
creature and swam ashore. What a surprise awaited him! There
was a military camp, soldiers and war machines. Sayed was
taken prisoner and brought before none other than Harun-el-
Rascid himself. The soldiers who had seized him said,

"Sire, this man must be one of the convicts that survived the
shipwreck."

"Is that so?" Harun-el-Rascid demanded gravely.

"Yes," replied Sayed, "I did survive the shipwreck. But I'm not a convict." And he explained how he had been reported to the police because of the bag of gold. "It was given to me," he went on, "by one of two men I saved one night from being attacked by four robbers." Harun-el-Rascid looked at the man sitting beside him and then said,

"Did the two men give you anything else?"

"Yes, they did, this ring," Sayed replied, showing the Caliph the ring which he kept round his neck with the whistle. Harun rose to his feet and exclaimed:

"Young man, the two men you helped were my chief minister and myself! Go free, but first tell me your name."

"Sayed, Sire."

"Sayed?" echoed the chief minister. "There's a man here in the camp called Benezar, who is searching for his son Sayed." "It's my father!" cried the young man. And it was his father. They hugged each other in delight.

Since justice must be done in the world, evil Kalum was arrested and imprisoned as he deserved to be . . .

THE EMPRESS JOWKA

Once upon a time . . . an Empress lived in Japan. She was young, beautiful, kindly, and wise, and her name was Jowka. She dreamt of living in peace, thinking of the welfare of her people, but in the northern mountains, a rebellion broke out led by Prince Kokai. He sent a message to the Empress,

"Jowka, either you must marry me and share the throne, or I will put your kingdom to the flame and sword!" Jowka, who knew that empresses never flinch at threats, replied,

"Kokai, we shall fight!", and sent an army against the rebels. The army was strong and well led and it defeated the rebels in more than one battle. But, just before the most important battle of all, something terrible and magical happened.

Kokai pleaded with one of the evil gods and it started to rain. The rivers grew swollen with water and broke their banks. There were appalling floods which took the Imperial army by surprise and swept it away. Every man, from the general to the humblest soldier, was drowned. And Kokai the rebel came down from the mountains and approached the capital of the Empire. Jowka sent other armies against him, but each one met the same fate: swept away in the swirling waters that obeyed Kokai's orders. The whole of Japan was terror-stricken. Was power to be seized by a merciless rebel magician?

Jowka was lost in thought over this when, one night, she heard a rustle in the room where she was saying her prayers. Lifting her eyes, she saw, standing in front of her, a man wearing a long tunic and holding a stick. He had long white hair and a flowing beard, as soft as silk. The Empress jumped in surprise, but the old man said:

"Have no fear, Jowka, I'm a friend. I'm the God of Fire. I heard your prayers, I know how much you are suffering, and I'm here to help. Don't worry! I shall join your armies and Kokai's magic will do nothing against me."

"Tell me, God of Fire, what must I do?" the Empress murmured.

"You must gather a new army to send against the rebel. I will march at the side of your general." And so the Empress ordered the greatest and biggest army ever seen in Japan to be mustered, and a huge number of men, horses and chariots set out.

Everyone, including the Imperial and the rebel soldiers, knew that the battle about to be fought would be final. The two opposing armies slowly drew closer on a vast plain, and the general leading the imperial troops murmured:

"It is unwise to march here. Kokai could easily flood this area!" The God of Fire, marching at the general's side in the guise of a bold young officer said:

"Have no fear, I'm far stronger than water." There were a few skirmishes, then Kokai, high on the mountain where he had made his camp, raised his arms invoking the help of the elements. The earth shook, there was a fierce gust of wind and an immense rush of water swept down the mountainside onto the plain. The Imperial soldiers screamed with terror, but the God of Fire simply said:

"Keep calm! That water will not even lap our feet." And indeed, the huge foaming waves that seemed to gallop towards the army, suddenly slowed down when they reached the God of Fire, drew back, split with a tremendous roar and were swallowed up by the earth.

"This is the end of Kokai! March on!" ordered the general, and the entire army marched on towards the mountain and defeated the enemy. Kokai saw that the rebellion was now over, his power had gone and his fortune too had disappeared. But rather than surrender to the Empress Jowka, who would have forgiven him, he hurled himself, head first, against the mountain and died. But the blow was so hard that the mountain, named Shu, cracked and from the crack gushed out fire, poisonous fumes and lava, that quickly invaded the plain below, burning and suffocating everything on it. A far worse danger now threatened the empire of the wise Jowka!

The Empress remained quite calm. Then she received another terrible piece of news. The crack in the mountain and the disaster that followed, had also cracked the pillars that held up the sky, damaging the pathway along which, every day, the Sun and the Moon travelled with their chariots, carrying the light.

In a short time, in fact, a dreadful dark shadow fell over all the world. People were afraid of the darkness, they wept and despaired. So wise Jowka ordered huge bonfires to be kept alight, so that the flames would give them comfort, courage and new hope. And she sent word to all her subjects that they should collect blue, white, black, orange and red stones and bring them to the palace. When that was done, the Empress ground down the stones, and made a kind of paste, something like liquid porcelain, transparent and shiny.

She put it in a pot, then with a magic spell summoned a cloud, climbed on top of it and made it carry her to the exact spot where the heavenly pillar was cracked. There, she repaired the damage using the strange coloured paste. As she went back to earth, she said to herself, "There! The pillar is mended. The chariots of the Sun and the Moon can take to the road again and the light will return." Alas! Things didn't quite happen that way! Days went by and the light had still not come back. The Sun and the Moon were nowhere to be seen. And the people, who had had such high hopes, again began to weep and wail. Everyone began to say, "Oh dear! We shall live the rest of our lives in the dark! We will go blind, we will die of the cold! Nothing will grow in the fields, and if we survive the dark and the cold, we will die of hunger!"

Once again, the Empress kept calm and was unworried. She called together all the wise men of the realm and asked them to find out what had happened. Long discussions took place, then a very learned philosopher went before Jowka and told her,

"Your most gracious Highness, I know exactly what has happened! When the pillar of heaven cracked, the Sun and the Moon shut themselves away in their palaces in alarm. And they have never come out again. How can they possibly know the pillar has been repaired?"

"Yes! Yes! That is so!" chorussed the other wise men. The Empress then said, "There is only one way to tell them. Send a messenger!"

"A messenger?" they asked. Jowka went on.

"Yes. Or rather, two! One to gallop to the Sun and the other to the Moon. We can't be discourteous, and if we were to warn one before the other, then the second one might take offence." All over the empire, a search was made for two horsemen brave enough to face such a long journey, and two horses strong enough to gallop into the heart of Day and Night. It wasn't easy to find suitable men but in the end, two young men came to Jowka, and she told them what had to be done . . .

The messengers set off. It was a long and fearful journey, from cloud to cloud, from heaven to heaven, through winds and storms, brushing past comets and shooting stars. But they delivered the Empress's message to the Sun and the Moon. The pillar had been repaired, their chariots could return to the heavenly pathways. The Sun and the Moon thanked the messengers.

The next day, the shadows disappeared from the daylight world, and light flooded back again, as before. The two messengers knelt before the Empress on their return, but Jowka made them rise to their feet, saying:

"No! Men like you shall always remain on their feet before anyone on earth, for you have looked the Sun and the Moon in the face!"

THE BOOK OF SPELLS

Once upon a time . . . in the middle of a forest round whose edges lay scattered some peasants cottages, an ogre used to live. He was big, cruel and heartless, but he liked his house to be tidy. So he said to himself,

"I'm always out hunting, fishing and causing trouble. I need somebody to look after the house, clean the floors, wash the plates and do the laundry every week . . ." Out he went and crouched down near one of the cottages, belonging to certain poor peasants.

When he saw their children come out, a boy and a girl, he stretched out his big hand, grabbed them and carried them away.

"You'll be my servants," he said, "and I will give you your food. But if you try to run away, you will be the next dish!" Terrified, the two children agreed, and they lived in the ogre's house for a long time. Then, they noticed that, every evening, the ogre pulled out a large book, which he would read carefully

. . . it was the Book of Spells! The two children, who were intelligent, read the book when the ogre was away, and they too learned the magic spells. At last, the boy said,

"Sister, I think I know enough now! Come on, let's run away!"

"Oh! Are you sure you know how to cast spells?" asked the girl anxiously.

"Of course!" said he. "Come on, before the ogre gets back!" So the pair ran out of the house and into the forest. Suddenly, the girl cried out,

"I can hear somebody running! The ogre's following us!" The ogre was determined to catch the pair and, without a doubt, with his long legs, he would soon catch up on them.

So the young lad cast the first of the spells. He turned himself into a pond and his sister into a minnow! A moment later, the ogre rushed up, saw what had taken place and growled:

"If only I had a line! I'll run and fetch one!" and off he went. The two children turned back into their normal selves and started to flee once more. But the ogre was soon on their heels and he was just about to lay hands on them, when the boy cast the second spell. He turned himself into a shrine and his sister into an angel painted on the wall. The ogre would have loved to kick the shrine to bits, but he didn't dare. He shouted,

"I'll burn you down instead!" and ran to fetch a bundle of wood.

In the meantime, however, the children were off again. They ran and ran, till they were exhausted and out of breath . . . And on the point of being snatched . . . the boy, working a third spell, turned himself and his sister into grains of corn, that mingled with thousands and thousands of other grains on the threshing floor . . . The ogre exclaimed:

"You think you can beat me with my own spells, but I'm far more cunning than you!" and he turned into a cockerel that hurriedly began to peck all the grains. What awful danger. But a second before being pecked, the boy turned into a fox, pounced on the cockerel and gobbled him up!

And now that the ogre was gone, the boy and his sister were able to go home again, safe and sound!

THE GAME OF CHESS

Once upon a time . . . in faraway Persia there was a King who had a beautiful wife and a handsome son called Gav. Life was all sunshine as far as he was concerned, but not for long.

One day, as he was going hunting, he fell from his horse and was killed. Women in Persia could not succeed to the throne and so the dead ruler's brother was proclaimed King. He was a prince called May. He fell in love with the widowed Queen and married her. She gave him a son whose name was Talend. Alas, some time later, the new King died and there only remained the Queen with the two sons, brothers of course, but with different fathers. The question was soon raised:–

"Which brother will become King of Persia?" "It will be Gav," was one reply, "because he is the elder." But others said, "It will be Talend, because he is the son of our last King." The Queen herself said nothing at all.

However, sooner or later, she would have to come to a decision, and she did not want to disappoint either Gav or Talend. As long as the two boys were small, it didn't matter, but when they started to grow up and began to ask when one or the other was going to be crowned King, the problems began. The Queen couldn't make up her mind. When her ministers asked her to make a choice, she would reply,

"Yes, I will do it tomorrow . . ." and so the years went by

Gav and Talend became young men, and rivals. As children they were always together, as youths, they saw little of each other, indeed, they kept out of each other's way. Each had his own set of friends. In that way, two sides were formed, one supporting Talend, the other supporting Gav. The ministers were very worried, and now insisted that the Queen choose the King. But she couldn't bring herself to do this, for fear of disappointing one of her dearly loved sons.

Some years later, the kingdom drifted towards what is known as civil war, for the two princes did not see eye to eye, neither wanted to give up the throne, neither wanted to step down. Some of the provinces sided with Talend, others with Gav. Certain battalions in the army swore allegiance to Talend, others to Gav. The two young men met, but only to stare at each other coldly and to promise war instead of peace, and war was fast approaching. Two opposing armies were built up, consisting of weapons, money, horses and elephants, very important in Persia, for they carried on their backs a wickerwork turret from which the archers fired arrows at the enemy. Gav's army began to march against Talend's. All Persia held its breath, awaiting the battle that was to decide its fate.

The battle was fought. Both armies had the same number of foot soldiers, horsemen, standard bearers and elephants. It was a terrible massacre. Neither of the brothers wanted the other to die. In spite of everything, the brothers felt the call of the family tie. Indeed, each had given an order that, if the soldiers found they were about to kill the enemy leader, they were to stop and warn him instead by shouting,

"Watch out, King!" The conflict lasted for a long time, until Gav's troops were overcome and Talend found himself with only a few soldiers to defend him. Then, a little later, quite alone, he found himself surrounded on all sides by Gav's turreted elephants, slowly advancing on him. No arrows were fired on the prince, he turned this way and that, searching for a way to escape, but his heart failed at that moment and he fell dead to the ground.

High in the palace tower, the Queen had watched the battle with sorrow in her heart, knowing full well that she was, at that moment, losing one of her sons. But which one? It didn't matter. She loved them both equally. When she saw that the dust had settled on the distant plain and the cries of battle had died away, the Queen came down from the tower and rushed through the palace to meet those returning from the field. She stopped in her tracks. Her son Gav, his clothes in tatters and splashed with blood, staggered sadly towards her.

"Talend?" stammered the Queen. Gav shook his head,

"Oh, mother," he said, "my brother Talend is dead."

"Dead! Did you kill him?"

"Oh, no, mother!" exclaimed Gav. "I would never have done such a thing."

"But you ordered his death!" exclaimed the Queen. The young man then knelt before her and, taking the hem of her dress in his hand, said,

"Mother, I swear nobody was responsible for my brother's death. He died, but not violently."

45

"I shall never believe that is the truth," wept the Queen. But Gav said,

"I shall prove that it is." He then thought of a way to show his mother how the battle had been fought. First of all, he asked a carpenter to make him a board, as flat as the plain. Then to mark the positions and manoeuvres of the two armies, the board was divided into white and black squares. A wood carver made him a miniature army of foot soldiers, a king, standard bearers, knights and towers, to take the place of the elephants and their turrets. When everything was ready, Gav called the Queen and, moving one piece at a time, acted out the various stages of battle.

"You see, mother, my foot soldiers advanced like this, so Talend manoeuvred his like that. Each time my brother was about to be killed, I had the men cry out 'watch out, King,' so that he could reach safety," said Gav.

"In the end, though, my Talend was no longer safe," murmured the Queen. Gav sadly replied,

"That's true. He was surrounded. But I would never have had him killed, mother. It was his heart that gave out. My brother realised he had lost, and so he died." The Queen then said,

"I understand, son, and I forgive you. I feel you'll be a good king for our country. But I wonder why, in a battle between two kings, one must win and the other lose . . ."

The poor Queen kept asking herself the same question for a very long time. She would sit all day long beside the little battlefield moving the pieces, foot soldiers, standard bearers and towers, always trying to save the King. In the end, she understood that, as in make-believe, so it is in real life, when there is a fight to the last, one of the opponents must fall, just as her son Talend had fallen.

One day, they found the poor Queen dead on what was, by then, known as the chessboard. That is how chess originated. Nowadays it is a peaceful contest that recalls a real-life battle. Today it is fun, but then it caused a poor mother who saw her sons fight against each other, sadness and suffering . . .

BLUEBEARD

Once upon a time . . . in the fair land of France, there lived a very rich and powerful lord, the owner of estates, farms and a great splendid castle, and his name was Bluebeard. This wasn't his real name, it was a nickname, due to the fact he had a long shaggy black beard with glints of blue in it. He was very handsome and charming, but, if the truth be told, there was something about him that made you feel respect, and a little uneasy . . .

Bluebeard often went away to war, and when he did, he left

his wife in charge of the castle . . . He had had lots of wives, all young, pretty and noble. As bad luck would have it, one after the other, they had all died, and so the noble lord was forever getting married again.

"Sire," someone would ask now and again, "what did your wives die of?"

"Hah, my friend," Bluebeard would reply, "one died of smallpox, one of a hidden sickness, another of a high fever, another of a terrible infection . . . Ah, I'm very unlucky, and they're unlucky too! They're all buried in the castle chapel," he added. Nobody found anything strange about that. Nor did the sweet and beautiful young girl that Bluebeard took as a wife think it strange either. She went to the castle accompanied by her sister Anna, who said:

"Oh, aren't you lucky marrying a lord like Bluebeard?"

"He really is very nice . . . and when you're close, his beard doesn't look as blue as folk say!" said the bride, and the two sisters giggled delightedly. Poor souls! They had no idea what lay in store for them! . . .

A month or so later, Bluebeard had the carriage brought round and said to his wife, "Darling, I must leave you for a few weeks. But keep cheerful during that time, invite whoever you like and look after the castle. Here," he added, handing his bride a bunch of keys, "you'll need these, the keys of the safe, the armoury and the library keys, and this one, which opens all the room doors. Now, this little key here," and he pointed to a key that was much smaller than the others, "opens the little room at the end of the great ground floor corridor. Take your friends wherever you want, open any door you like, but not this one! Is that quite clear?" repeated Bluebeard. "Not this one! Nobody at all is allowed to enter that little room. And if you ever did go into it, I would go into such a terrible rage that it's better that you don't!"

"Don't worry, husband," said Bluebeard's wife as she took the keys, "I'll do as you say." After giving her a hug, Bluebeard got into his carriage, whipped up the horses and off he went.

The days went by. The young girl invited her friends to the castle and showed them round all the rooms except the one at the end of the corridor.

"Why shouldn't I see inside the little room? Why? Why is it forbidden?" Well, she thought about it so much that she ended up bursting with curiosity, until one day she opened the door and walked into the little room . . . Of all the ghastly horrors! Inside, hanging on the walls were the bodies of Bluebeard's wives; he had strangled them all with his own hands!

Terror stricken, the girl ran out of the room, but the bunch of keys slipped from her grasp. She picked them up without a glance and hurried to her own room, her heart thumping wildly in her chest. Horrors! She was living in a castle of the dead! So that is what had happened to Bluebeard's other wives!

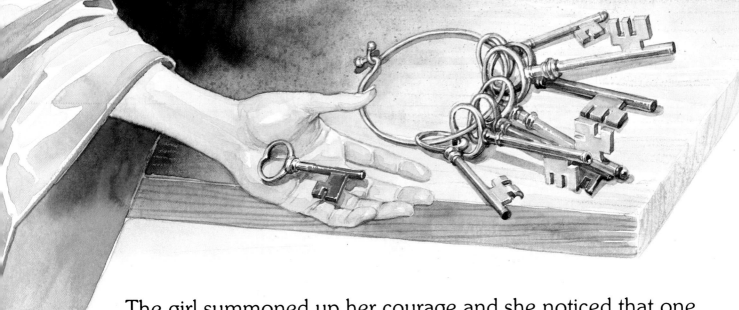

The girl summoned up her courage and she noticed that one of the keys – the very key to the little room – was stained with blood.

"I must wipe it clean, before my husband comes back!" she said to herself. But try as she would, the blood stain wouldn't wash away. She washed, she scrubbed and she rinsed it; all in vain, for the key was still red. That very evening, Bluebeard came home. Just imagine the state his poor wife was in!

Bluebeard did not ask his wife for the keys that same evening, but he remarked:

"You look a little upset, darling. Has anything nasty happened?"

"Oh, no! No!"

"Are you sorry I came back so soon?"

"Oh, no! I'm delighted!" But that night, the bride didn't sleep a wink. Next day, Bluebeard said:

"Darling, give me back the keys," and his wife hurriedly did so. Bluebeard remarked: "There's one missing, the key to the little room!"

"Is there?" said the young girl, shaking,

"I must have left it in my room!"

"All right, go and get it." But when Bluebeard's wife put the key into his hand, Bluebeard turned white and in a deep hoarse voice demanded:

"Why is this key stained with blood?"

"I don't know . . ." stammered his wife.

"You know very well!" he retorted. "You went into the little room, didn't you? Well, you'll go back again, this time for good, along with the other ladies in there. You must die!"

"Oh no! I pray you!"

"You must die!" he repeated. Just then, there was a knock at the door and Anna, Bluebeard's wife's sister, entered the castle.

"Good morning," she said, "you seem rather pale."

"Not at all, we're quite well," replied Bluebeard. His wife whispered in his ear:

"Please, please give me ten minutes to live!" Bluebeard replied:

"No more than ten!" The girl ran to her sister Anna who had gone up to one of the towers and asked her,

"Anna, do you see our brothers coming? They promised they would come and see me today!" But Anna replied:

"No, I don't see anyone. What's wrong? You look agitated"

"Anna, please," said the shaken girl, "look again! Are you sure you can't see someone?"

"No," said her sister, "only one or two peasants." Just then the voice of Bluebeard boomed up to them:

"Wife, your time is up! Come here!"

"I'm coming!" she called, but then said to her sister: "Oh Anna, aren't our brothers coming? . . ."

"No," replied Anna. Again Bluebeard shouted up.

"Come down at once! Or I'll come up!" Trembling like a leaf,

his wife went downstairs. Bluebeard was clutching a big knife and he grabbed his bride by the hair . . .

"Sister, I can see two horsemen coming!" called out Anna from the tower that very moment. Bluebeard made a horrible face:

"They too will die!" His wife knelt to implore:

"Please, please don't kill me. I'll never tell anyone what I saw! I'll never say a word!"

"Yes, you'll never say a word for eternity!" snarled Bluebeard, raising the knife. The poor girl screamed:

"Have pity on me!" But he fiercely replied:

"No! You must die!" He was about to bring the knife down on the girl's delicate neck, when two young men burst into the room: a dragoon and a musketeer. They were his wife's brothers.

Drawing their swords, they leapt towards Bluebeard, who tried to flee up some stairs, but was caught and killed. And that was the end of the sad story. Bluebeard's poor wives were given a Christian burial, the castle was completely renovated and the young widow, some time later, married a good and honest young man, who helped her to forget her terrible adventure. And that young lady completely lost all her sense of curiosity . . .